LIGHT

The Rosen Publishing Group's
PowerKids Press™
New York

Ian F. Mahaney

Published in 2007 by the Rosen Publishing Group, Inc.
29 East 21st Street, New York, NY 10010

First Edition

Editor: Joanne Randolph
Book Design: Julio Gil

Photo Credits: Cover, title page © Lawrence Manning/Corbis; p. 4 © RNT Productions/Corbis; p. 5 © Paula Bronstein/Getty Images; p. 6 © Randy Lincks/Corbis; p. 8 © Artville; p. 9 © David Sacks/Getty Images; p. 12 © Bettmann/Corbis; p. 15 © Frans Lanting/Corbis; p. 16 © Eyewire; p. 18 © Roy Morsch/Corbis; p. 19 Courtesy NASA/JPL-Caltech; pp. 20, 21, 22 The Rosen Publishing Group.

Library of Congress Cataloging-in-Publication Data

Mahaney, Ian F.
  Light / Ian F. Mahaney.— 1st ed.
      p. cm. — (Energy in action)
  Includes index.
  ISBN (10) 1-4042-3476-4 (13) 978-1-4042-3476-5 (lib. bdg.) —
ISBN (10) 1-4042-2185-9 (13) 978-1-4042-2185-7 (pbk.)
  1. Light—Juvenile literature. I. Title. II. Energy in action (PowerKids Press)
  QC360.M35 2007
  535—dc22
                                        2005029478

Manufactured in the United States of America

CONTENTS

What Is Energy?

Sometimes when you wake up in the morning after a great night's sleep, you may feel full of energy. What does it mean to be full of energy? Having energy means you have the ability to do something active. Another way of saying this is that you have the ability to do work. It can be homework or lifting a heavy box.

Forms of energy include **mechanical**, electrical, **chemical**, and thermal, or heat, energy. People get energy from food. A lamp gets energy from electricity. A plant gets energy from light.

Opposite: Swimming is one way a person uses energy. *Above:* A person must use energy to do work. Here boxes are being loaded onto a truck. The person doing the work uses chemical energy from stored food. As the box is moved, it has mechanical energy.

Light Is a Form of Energy

Light is all around us. We see and use light every day, so let's **investigate** what light is.

Light is a form of energy that makes eyesight possible. Light **reflects** off objects and hits our eyes. Our brains turn the information from the light into a picture.

Light is made up of photons. Photons are tiny packets of energy. Sometimes light is described as moving in a straight line, like bullets. Light is also described as moving in waves, like ocean waves. Light waves come in many different sizes and **frequencies**.

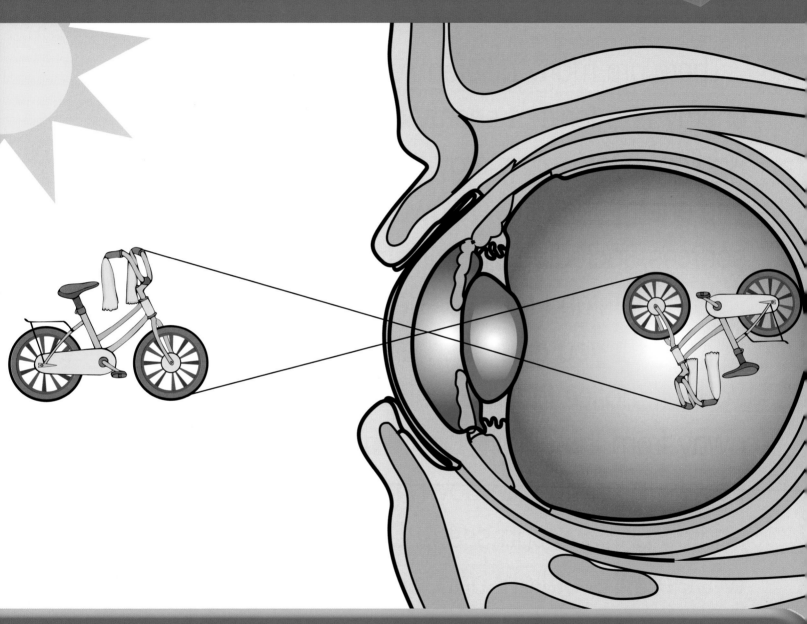

Opposite: A campfire provides light outdoors. The light energy is created by the reaction between heat and wood. *Above:* We can see objects because light hits them and is reflected into our eye. Here an image of a bike passes through the curved lens of the eye and hits the back of the eye. The image is upside-down in the eye. The brain translates this information, and we see the bike right side up.

7

Light Is Radiant Energy

There are many different forms of energy. Light energy is a form of energy called **radiant energy**. Radiant energy is energy that is given off by a **source**. The energy then travels away from the source. All light sources, including the Sun, radiate their energy.

To understand radiant energy, think about what happens if you drop a small object into a pot of water. You will notice that the water ripples, or makes waves, away from the object. Light travels in waves, too. Light travels in an up-and-down motion from the source until we can see it. Different wavelengths of light appear to our eyes as different colors.

In both these images, you can see the idea of radiant energy. As an object, such as a raindrop or a rock, hits the surface of the water, waves ripple out in all directions from this point. This is how radiant energy works, too.

The Science of Light

To study how light is created, we first need to look at an **atom**. An atom is a tiny **particle** that is made up of matter. Everything, from your skin to your desk, is made up of atoms. An atom is made up of three parts called **protons**, **neutrons**, and **electrons**. Electrons travel around the center, or **nucleus**, of an atom.

Electrons travel around the nucleus at a fixed distance. However, an atom can be energized, usually by heating it. This can send an electron farther away from the nucleus. As the electron drops back to its usual position it gives off a photon.

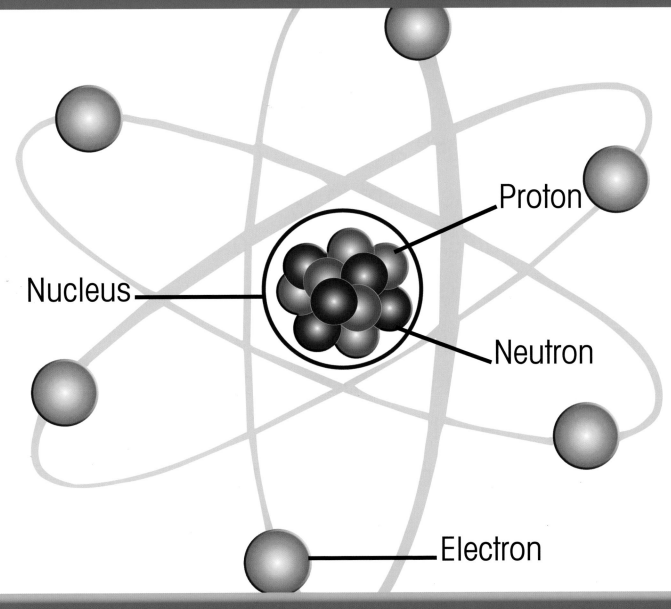

Proton

Nucleus

Neutron

Electron

This is a drawing of an atom. You can see the electrons in red. The protons are green and the neutrons are blue. The yellow ovals stand for the path the electrons take as they spin around the nucleus.

What Does Light Look Like?

Ordinary, uncolored light is called white light. Did you know that white light is actually made up of many colors, though? A scientist named Isaac Newton did an experiment in which he broke apart white light into different colors. Breaking light into its different colors is called **refraction**.

To conduct his experiment, Newton directed a beam of light into a dark room and through a clear glass **prism**. The light broke apart into many colors. These colors are called the **spectrum**. Newton then recombined the spectrum of colors into white light by shining the colors through a second prism. This proved that white light includes many colors.

Red   Orange   Yellow   Green   Blue   Violet

Visible Light

Infrared   Ultraviolet   X-rays   Gamma Rays

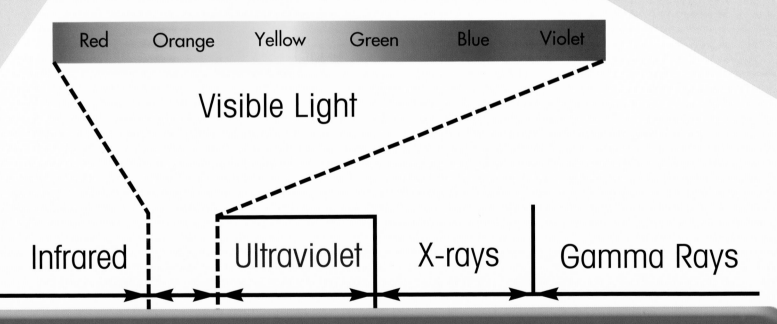

Opposite: This color drawing shows Newton doing his light experiment. *Above:* There are many kinds of light, as shown in this diagram. The only light we can see is visible light. Though we cannot see ultraviolet light, we need to wear sunscreen to keep our skin safe from these rays. X-rays are used to take pictures of our bones.

13

A Rainbow

Refraction of light occurs naturally. You have probably seen examples of this yourself. Often at the end of a rainstorm, the Sun will appear and its light shines through the raindrops. The raindrops act like the prism in Newton's experiment. The water breaks apart, or refracts, the sunlight and you can see the colors of the spectrum. This is called a rainbow. Red, orange, yellow, green, blue, indigo, and violet are the colors you may see in a rainbow. The next time you see a rainbow, you can explain to your friends that the white light from the Sun has been broken into many colors by the raindrops.

A rainbow is a natural refraction of white light into its many colors. Have you ever heard of Roy G. Biv? Roy G. Biv is not a person but a way to help you remember the order of the colors in the spectrum. The *I* stands for indigo, a color between blue and violet.

The Visible Spectrum and Color

Light we can see is called the visible spectrum. There is also much radiant energy that we cannot see. Some examples are X-rays and radio waves.

When light hits an object, the color that we see is due to the colors in light. Sometimes light is scattered. For example, when sunlight hits Earth, the blue part of the spectrum is scattered across the sky, making it look blue. Sometimes an object **absorbs** the colors in light. We see the object in the colors that are reflected back. The leaves on a tree absorb the red waves of light and reflect back blue and yellow. Together yellow and blue appear green to our eyes.

Opposite: The sky appears blue and the grass green because of the colors that are absorbed or reflected. *Above:* This diagram shows that an apple appears red because it absorbs all the colors of the spectrum except for red. The red is reflected from the apple's surface, so the apple looks red to our eye.

The Sun

The Sun is our most important source of light energy. The Sun is a collection of burning gases that is 93,000,000 miles (150,000,000 km) from Earth.

Only a tiny amount of the light created by the Sun ever reaches Earth. Yet that light is enough light to make life possible on Earth. People have also **imitated** sunlight by making **artificial** light. Artificial light, such as the lightbulbs that light up your classroom, helps us see when the Sun is not shining. We use sunlight and artificial light for so many purposes. Can you think of other ways that we use light?

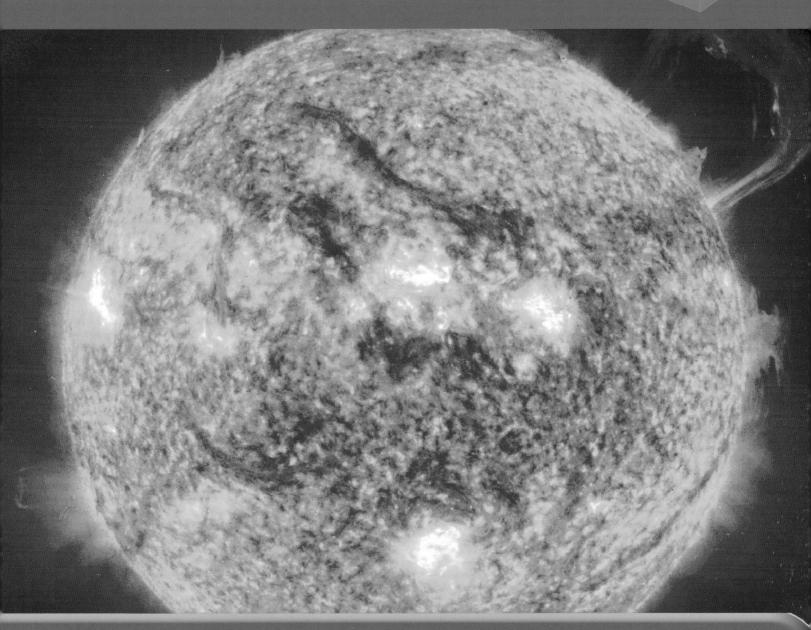

Opposite: A small tree grows in the sunlight. Without sunlight this plant could not create the food it needs to live. *Above:* The Sun produces a huge amount of light and heat. The Sun's surface is about 10,000° F (5,500° C) and its center is about 27 million° F (15 million° C).

Experiments with Light: Reflecting Light

You see objects because light reflects off them. Different surfaces reflect light in different ways. One way to see with reflected light is through a periscope. When a submarine is underwater, a periscope is used to see what's happening on the surface.

Step 1 To make a periscope, cut two thin, diagonal, or sloping, openings on opposite sides of a cardboard milk or juice carton. Use a ruler to place the openings, then draw two lines. Cut the openings.

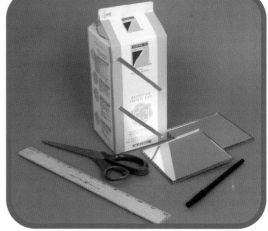

Step 2 Carefully push a mirror into the top opening so that the

mirror side faces down. Push a mirror into the bottom opening so that the mirror side faces up.

Step 3 On the front of the carton, cut out a square opening so that it's facing the top mirror.

Step 4 Punch a hole with a sharpened pencil into the back of the carton near the bottom mirror. Standing near a corner, hold the carton so that only the square looks out from the corner. Peek into the small hole. What do you see? You should be able to see images from around the corner.

Experiments with Light: Bending Light

Sometimes light rays bend when they pass through certain matter or objects. For example, light rays bend when they pass from air to water. This bending is called refraction. Refraction is a property of light that is very useful. We used curved pieces of glass called lenses to refract light to help people see better. Glasses and telescopes are two examples of this. Here's an experiment to try.

Step 1 Rest a spoon at an angle in a glass of water.

Step 2 Stand back and look at the glass. The spoon appears to bend into two sections. This is because the light rays bend as they pass from water into air. The bending light rays make the spoon look as though it is bending, too.

Glossary

absorbs (ub-ZORBZ) Takes in and holds on to something.

artificial (ar-tih-FIH-shul) Made by people, not nature.

atom (A-tem) The smallest part of an element that can exist either alone or with other elements.

chemical (KEH-mih-kul) Having to do with matter that can be mixed with other matter to cause changes.

electrons (ih-LEK-tronz) Particles inside atoms that spin around the nucleus. They have a negative charge.

frequencies (FREE-kwent-seez) The number of waves per second.

imitated (IH-muh-tayt-ed) Copied something or someone.

investigate (in-VES-tih-gayt) To try to learn the facts about something.

mechanical (mih-KA-nih-kul) Having to do with the physical science that deals with energy and forces and their effect on things.

neutrons (NOO-tronz) Particles with a neutral electric charge found in the nucleus of atoms.

nucleus (NOO-klee-us) Protons and neutrons joined together in the center of an atom.

particle (PAR-tih-kul) A small piece of something.

prism (PRIH-zuhm) A block of glass that separates white light into the colors of the rainbow.

protons (PROH-tonz) Particles with a positive electric charge found in the nucleus of atoms.

radiant energy (RAY-dee-ent EH-nur-jee) Energy that is carried by a wave.

reflects (rih-FLEKTS) Throws back light, heat, or sound.

refraction (rih-FRAK-shun) Something, such as a light ray or sound waves, that is bent away from a straight path.

source (SORS) The place from which something starts.

spectrum (SPEK-trum) The colors of the rainbow, or the colors formed when light passes through a prism.

Index

A

atom(s), 10

C

color(s), 8, 12, 14, 16

M

matter, 10

N

Newton, Isaac, 12, 14

P

photon(s), 6, 10
prism, 12, 14

R

radiant energy, 8, 16
refraction, 12, 14

S

spectrum, 12, 14, 16
Sun, 8, 14, 18

W

white light, 12, 14

Web Sites

Due to the changing nature of Internet links, PowerKids Press has developed an online list of Web sites related to the subject of this book. This site is updated regularly. Please use this link to access the list: www.powerkidslinks.com/eic/light/